Mess MONsters in the Garden

Beth Shoshan

Illustrated by
Piers Harper

Albury Children's

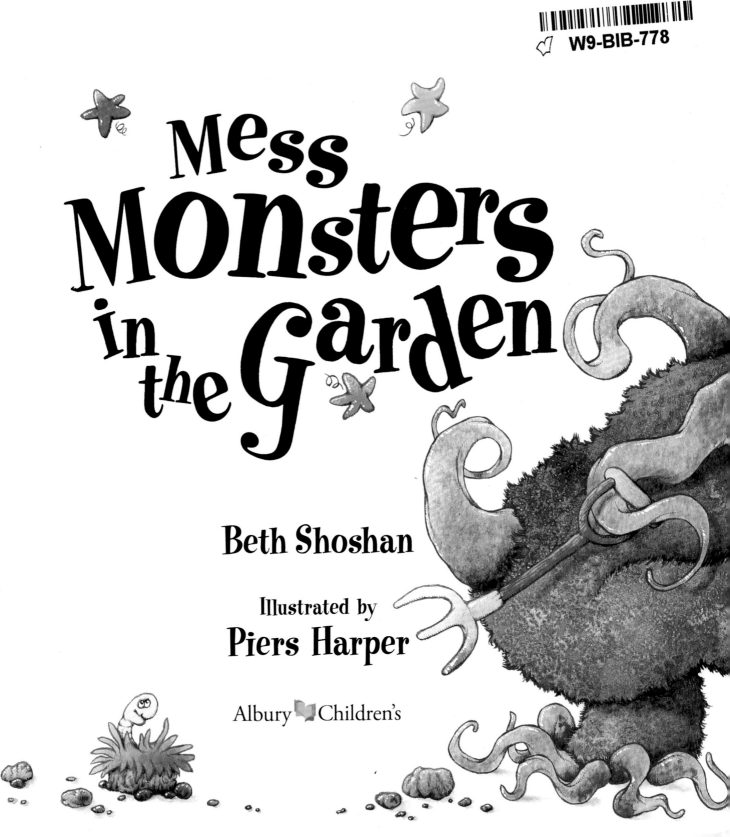

One day Mommy said
"The garden's a mess!"
And because it's so dirty
She suffers from stress.

I said,

"we need the dirt,
It's better – I know,
If it's tidy and clean
Then nothing will grow!"

But Mommy said "Nonsense!

That cannot be right!

I want nice paths and decking

And things to delight!"

What she didn't know
Was that locked in the shed
Was a big gang of monsters
From under my bed...

She'd told them

to clear out,

skedaddle,
skiddoO!

To stop messing my room up

As they used to do.

First a **hook,** then a **Crook,**

What a **hideous** sight,

As my **MOB** of Mess Monsters *crashed* into the light!

Those **monstrous monsters burst** up through the ground,

Shouting and
screaming
with
ear-splitting
sounds.

They **churned** and **upturned** the soil and the earth,

Throwing mud all about them for all it was worth.

Even Teddy was ready

To lend them a paw.

But they **trashed** him

and **s*tom*ped** him,

And left him quite sore.

They dug up some toys
I was sure I had lost.
Then **crushed** them,

and **mashed** them,
Which made me quite cross.

I'd seen quite enough,

So I shouted,

Oi!

Stop!

And I handed a spade

To the monster on top...

So with bucket and fork
And a long garden hose,
Trying to avoid
any thorns in their toes,

They started to dig up
All over the place,
Throwing plants everywhere,
Getting mud in their face.

They scrabbled and scrambled
And worked through the night.

And when morning was here...

...what a fabulous sight!

Because...

Mommy was wrong

(Though we daren't tell her so!).

It's the mess in the garden

That makes gardens grow!

For

My Mommy
B.S.

For

Kate, Tim, Dan, Nick and Sadie
P.H.

Published by Albury Books in 2014
Albury Court, Albury, Thame,
OX9 2LP, United Kingdom

ISBN 978-1-909958-41-8 (hardback)
ISBN 978-1-909958-20-3 (paperback)

A CIP catalogue record for this
book is available from the British Library
10 9 8 7 6 5 4 3
Printed in China